THE TIME TRAVELLERS

Welsh History Activity Book

TANWEN HAF

ILLUSTRATIONS
TELOR GWYN

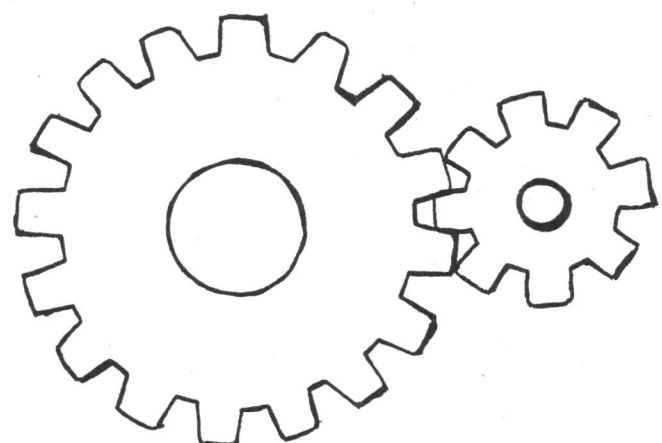

MY HISTORY

A family tree is a chart showing family relationships. Here is Princess Gwenllian's family tree. It shows Gwenllian herself, her parents and, on the top row, her grandparents.

Today, everyone's births, deaths and marriages are recorded, but in the past only the rich and powerful would do this, by creating a family tree scroll called a "pedigree" to prove how important they were. Sometimes, they weren't entirely honest!

Cynan ab Iago
PRINCE OF GWYNEDD

Died 1060

Ragnailt ingen Amlaíb

Married 1036
Dublin, Ireland

Died 1076

Owain ab Edwyn
PRINCE OF GWYNEDD

Died 1105

Morwyl ferch Ednywain
PRINCESS OF DEHEUBARTH

Born 1049
Tegeingl, Wales

Gruffudd ap Cynan
PRINCE OF GWYNEDD

Born c. 1055
Dublin, Ireland

Died 1137

Angharad ferch Owain

Born c. 1065

Married c. 1095

Died 1162

Gwenllian ferch Gruffudd
PRINCESS OF DEHEUBARTH

Born c. 1100
Aberffraw, Anglesey, Wales

Died 1136

Gwenllian lived a long time ago, so we don't know exactly when her birthday was.

The c. stands for "*circa*", which is Latin for "around". This is used when you are not sure of the exact date.

Here is a basic family tree chart.
Can you fill in the details, starting at the bottom with your name?

It doesn't matter if you don't have all the facts about your family. Ask them what they know.
They might not have all the answers, but there are bound to be some interesting stories.
You could do some detective work to find out more about your family tree by
searching old records for clues. Your local library can be a great place to start.

You may want to include more parents, grandparents and half or step brothers and sisters.
If so, you can copy this sheet, or draw your own chart.

3

WHO'S WHO?

Here are a few characters from Welsh history. Can you match the name to the picture?
Write the numbers in the circles next to each name.

- ◯ Alfred Russel Wallace
- ◯ Abram Wood
- ◯ Betty Campbell
- ◯ Black Bart
- ◯ Dic Penderyn
- ◯ Eileen Beasley
- ◯ Frances Hoggan
- ◯ Gwenllian ferch Gruffudd
- ◯ Henry Morgan
- ◯ Joan Curran
- ◯ Lyn Evans
- ◯ Owain Glyndŵr
- ◯ Margaret Tisdale
- ◯ Mr Urdd

WHICH HAPPENED FIRST?

Here are some significant events from Welsh history.
Can you label the events with the correct year?

948	1258	1839	1919	1991
c. 1100	1415	1858	1952	1999
1176	1672	1884	1966	2001

Answers on page 31.

1. Eileen Beasley refuses to pay her rate bill

2. 500 Welsh archers and 23 men-at-arms fight at Agincourt, France

3. Alfred Russel Wallace writes to Darwin outlining his theory of natural selection

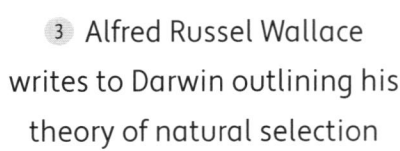

4. Race Riots in south Wales

5. Death of Hywel Dda (Hywel ap Cadell)

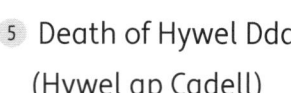

6. Colin Charvis becomes the first black captain of the Welsh rugby team

7. Bangor University is founded

FARMING

Early humans were hunter-gatherers, before they started herding livestock.
It was only when people started growing crops that they settled down and built farms.

Farming is an important part of the Welsh economy today, and it's not just the farmers hard at work. But . . . the farmer's dog is missing!

Can you help herd the sheep through the maze and into the pen?

The dairy, or milk, industry is an important part of Welsh farming today. But cows produce a lot of poo... The combination of manure and water washed out of the barn is called slurry.

MATHEMOOTICS!

Each cow produces 50 litres of slurry every day!

That is around [ ] litres every 30 days.

During the winter, cows are normally kept indoors and farmers have to be able to store 4 months' (120 days) worth of waste.

So the farmer needs to have enough storage space for [ ] litres per cow.

The average size of the Welsh dairy herd is 95 cows.

The farmer therefore needs space for [ ] litres of slurry!

Slurry can be used as fertilizer by spreading it on the fields when the weather is better. In this way, it prevents it polluting our rivers. As you can see, it's really important that farmers know how to do their maths!

Did you know that cows can produce up to 9,000 litres of milk a year? If you have 200ml of milk on your cereal, one cow could supply enough milk for [ ] bowls of cereal a year!

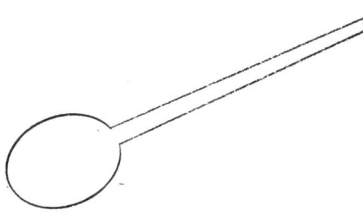

If you have one bowl of cereal every day, that would be [ ] litres of milk every year.

Tea is traditionally drunk in Wales, but everyone makes it differently. How much milk do the following people have in their cuppas every day? Write the answers in the cups.

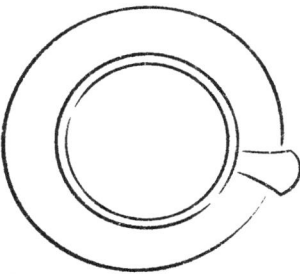

Jac likes his tea strong. He only takes 5ml of milk in his tea and drinks 6 cups a day.

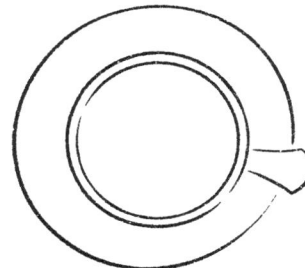

Sioned likes her tea milky. She takes 20ml of milk and drinks 10 cups a day.

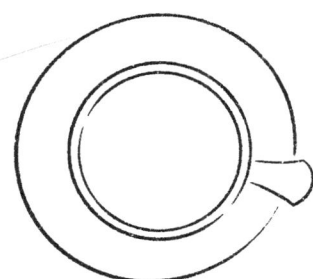

Bethan takes 12ml of milk in her cuppa, and drinks 5 cups a day.

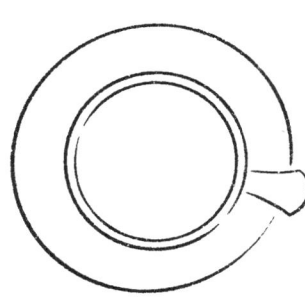

Mei prefers coffee, and drinks 3 cups a day with 50ml of milk.

Answers on page 31.

THE SHAPE OF HISTORY

The Bronze Age began around 2,500 BCE. The people of Britain made metal tools out of copper and bronze dug out of mines. Trade developed with the rest of Europe.

This Roman soldier has gone dotty!

The first record we have of people living in the area covered by present-day Wales dates from 54 BCE. A tribe living in the north-east of Wales helped to fight off an invasion by the forces of the Roman Emperor, Julius Caesar.

The Romans struggled to conquer the western part of Britain at first. It took 13 campaigns before they eventually captured the last remaining stronghold, Anglesey.

Between the years 383 and 410, the Roman Legions withdrew from Britain.

After the Romans left, Anglo-Saxons, Germanic tribes, moved to Britain and settled in England. During the 5th and 6th centuries, they fought to control more land and pushed back the Welsh border.

But the Romans didn't leave without a trace. There is evidence of Roman settlement in many parts of Wales.

Among them are the remains of several Roman fortresses, including Isca at Caerleon, Trawsgoed near Aberystwyth, and Segontium in Caernarfon.

Roman roads linked the fortresses. The best known example is Sarn Helen, which stretches 160 miles all the way from Caerhun in Conwy, to Carmarthen.

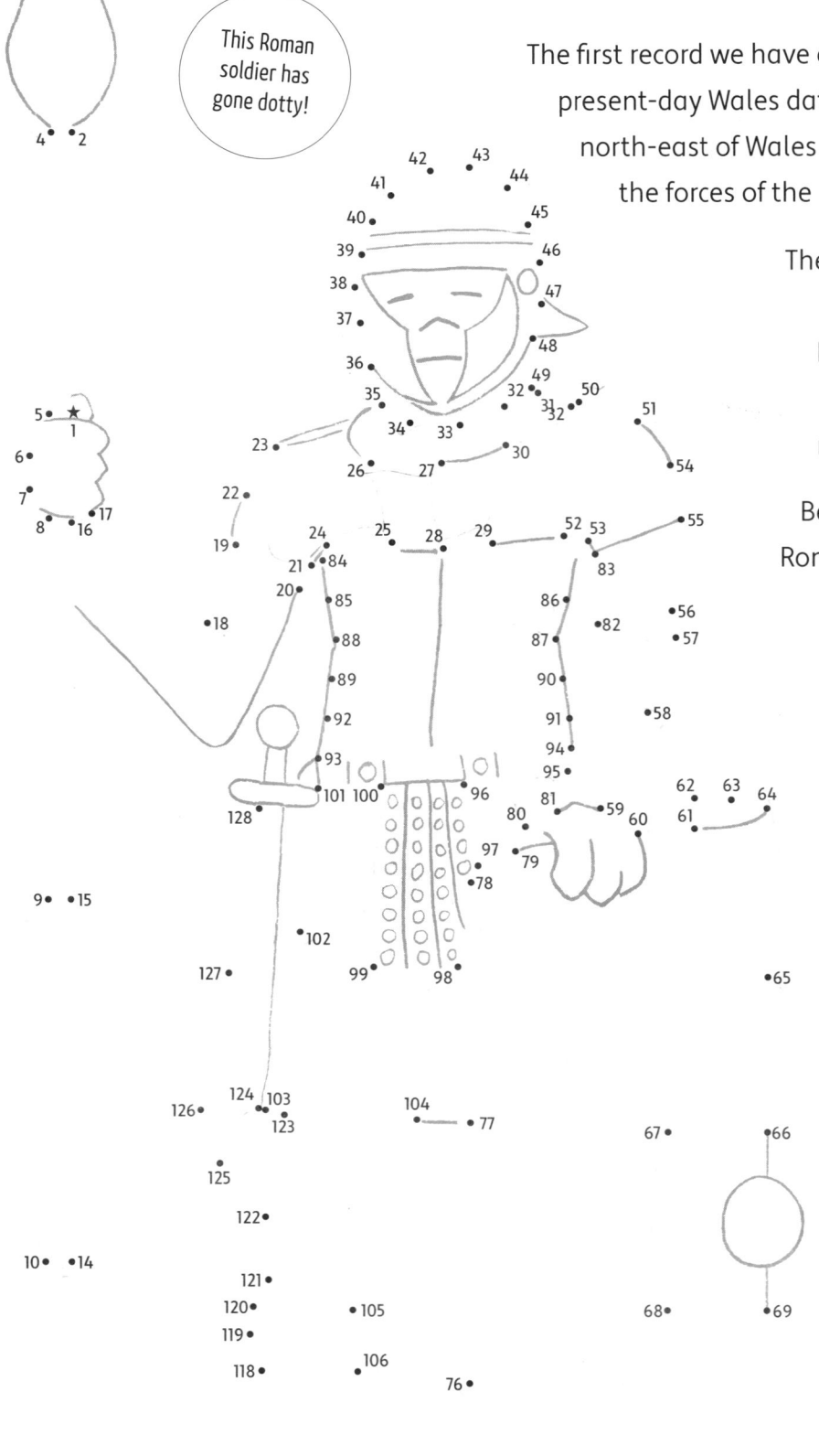

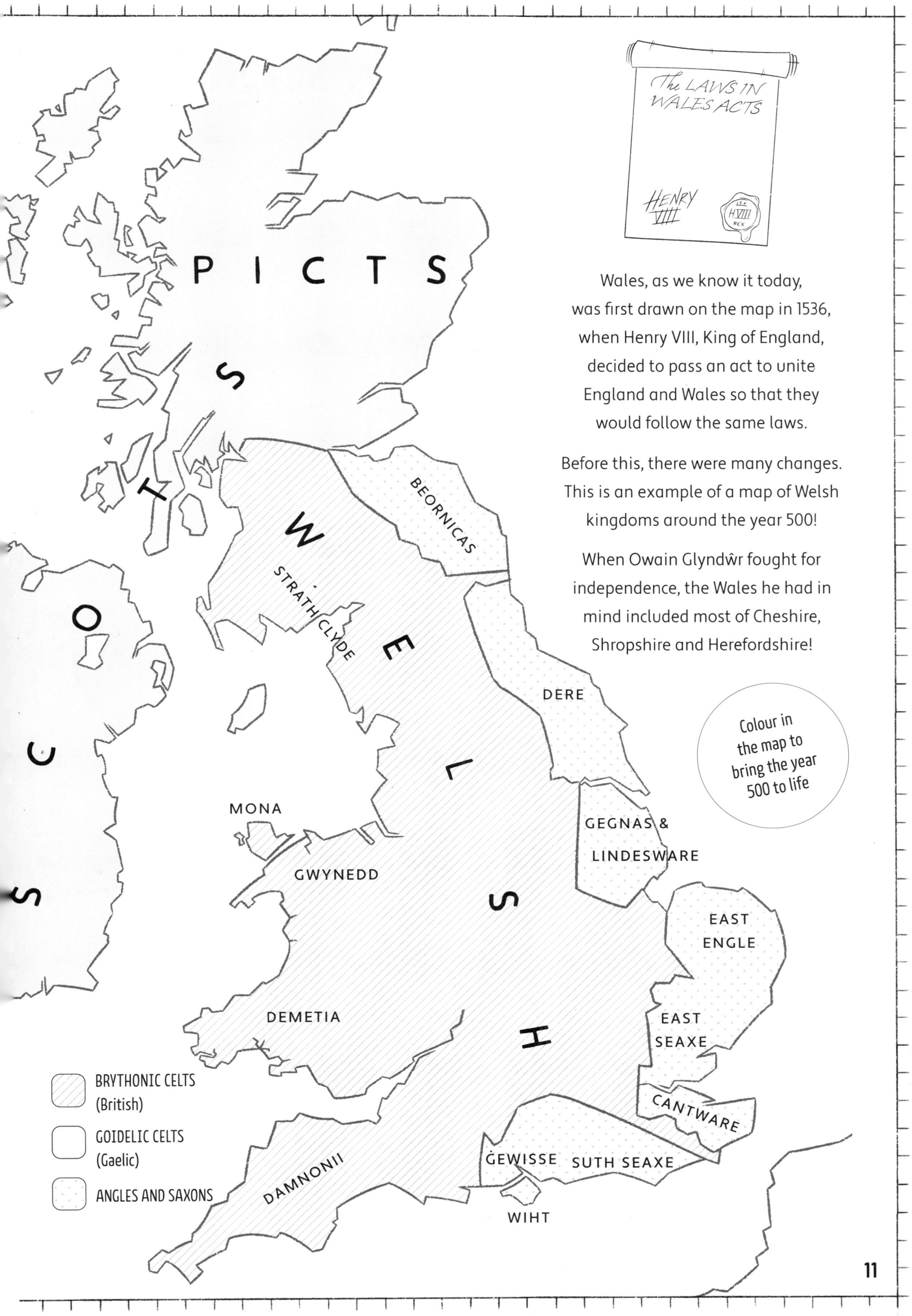

DEFENDING WALES

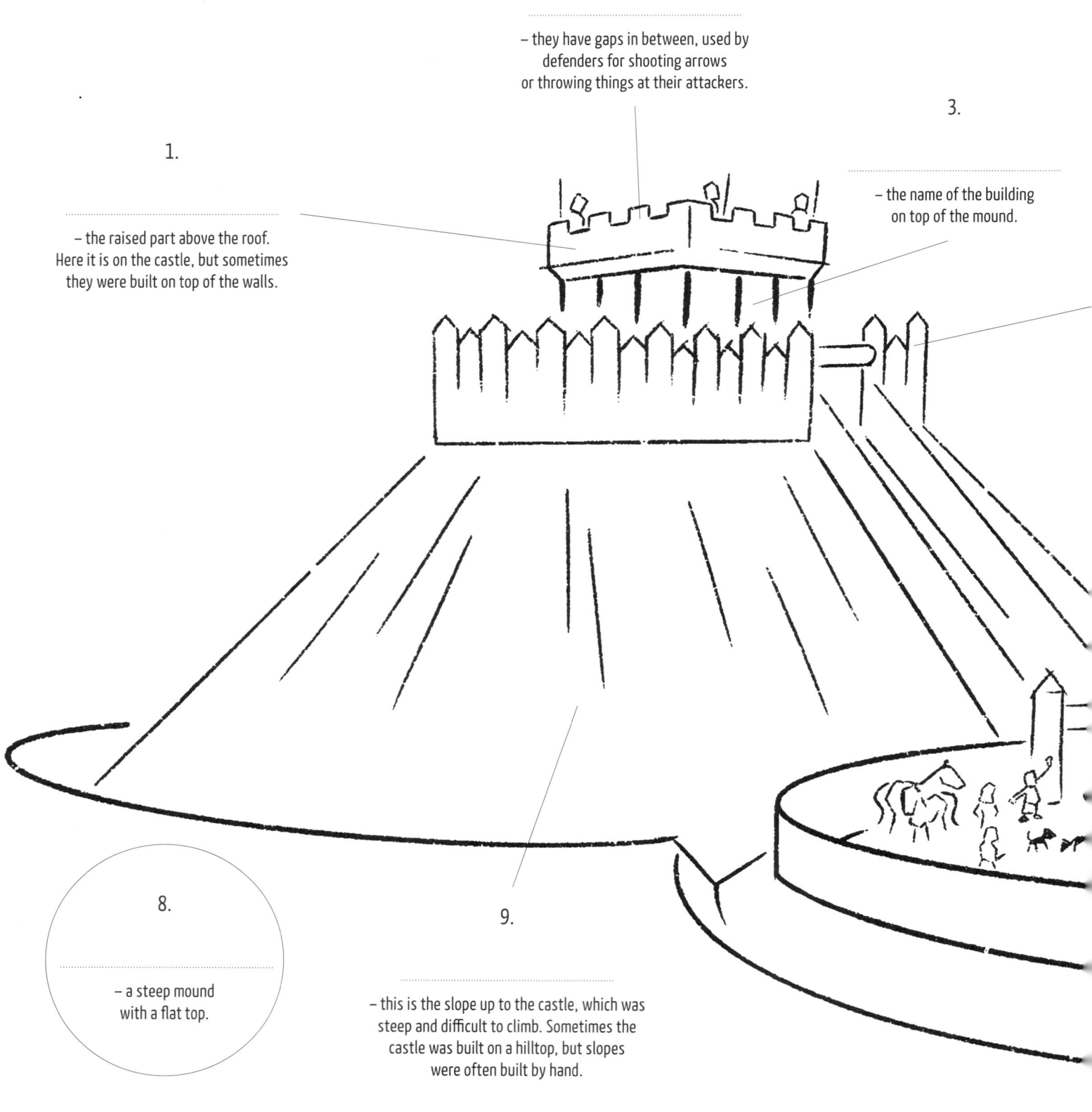

2.
– they have gaps in between, used by defenders for shooting arrows or throwing things at their attackers.

3.
– the name of the building on top of the mound.

1.
– the raised part above the roof. Here it is on the castle, but sometimes they were built on top of the walls.

8.
– a steep mound with a flat top.

9.
– this is the slope up to the castle, which was steep and difficult to climb. Sometimes the castle was built on a hilltop, but slopes were often built by hand.

There are many castles in Wales, some of them built by Welsh people, and some built by invaders to keep the Welsh out.

The castles sometimes changed hands after a battle, were demolished and rebuilt in a different style. Many castles built in Wales were motte-and-bailey castles. Here is a diagram showing all the different parts and their purpose.

Can you write the labels in the correct places on the diagram?

The descriptions underneath will give you a clue.

BAILEY   DRAWBRIDGE   MOTTE
BATTLEMENT   GREAT HALL   PALISADE
CURTAIN WALL   KEEP   PARAPET
DITCH or MOAT   MAIN GATE   SCARP

Answers on page 31.

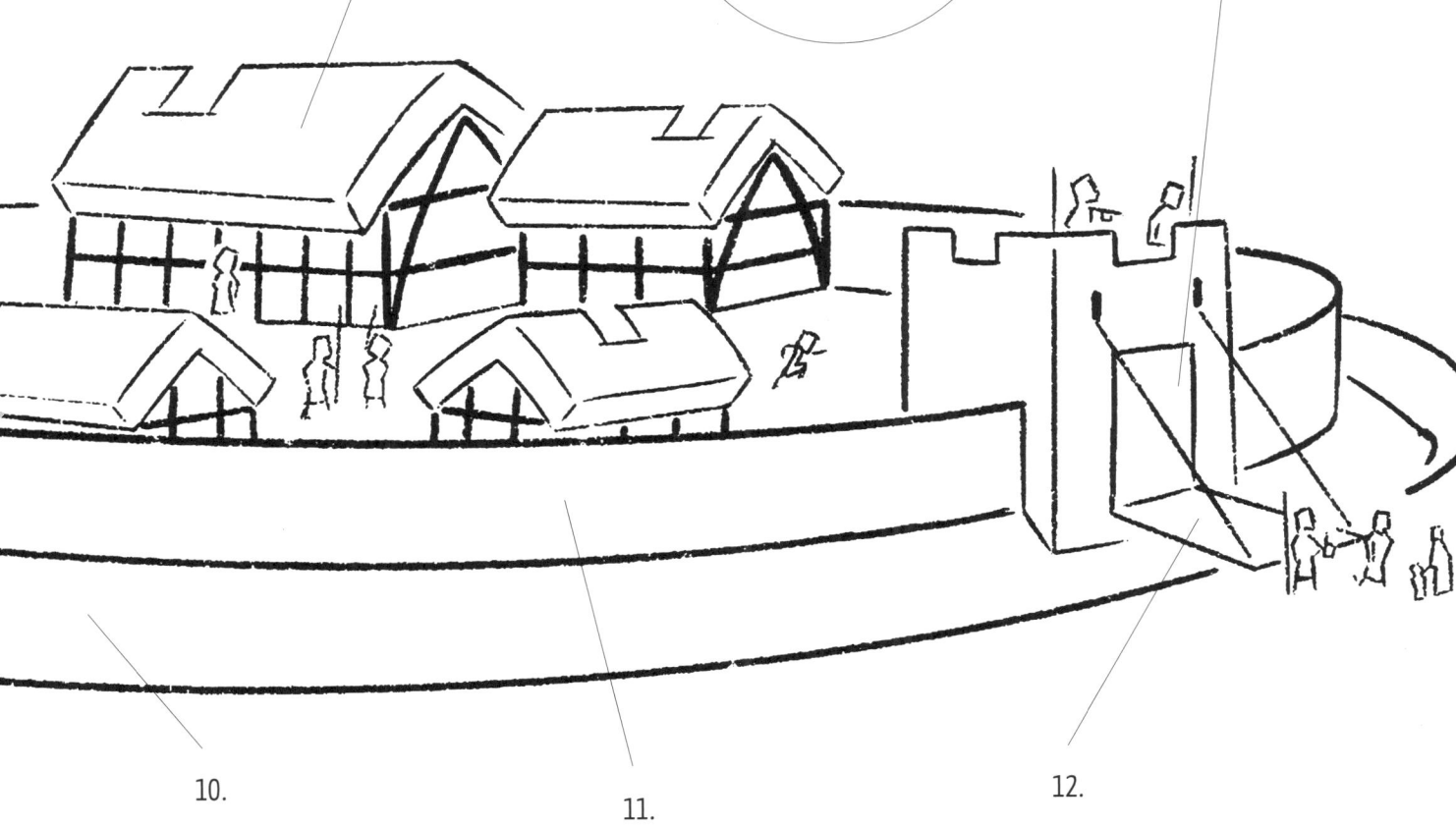

4. – a wall made from wooden stakes.

5. – can you imagine the feasts and parties a leader might hold to celebrate a victory in battle?

6. – this is the name for the courtyard which is surrounded by a curtain wall.

7. – the main entrance to the castle. The guards are keeping an eye on anyone who comes near.

10. – to make it harder for anyone to attack the walls.

11. – for keeping the people safe from attack. Older castles sometimes had palisade walls, which might later be replaced with stone walls.

12. – can be lowered to let people in, or raised to prevent entry.

13

BUILD YOUR OWN CASTLE

What was it like to live in a castle?
It wasn't only soldiers who lived here.
Their families were here, together with
many workers including blacksmiths
and carpenters, and animals too.
I'm sure life could be quite "colourful"!

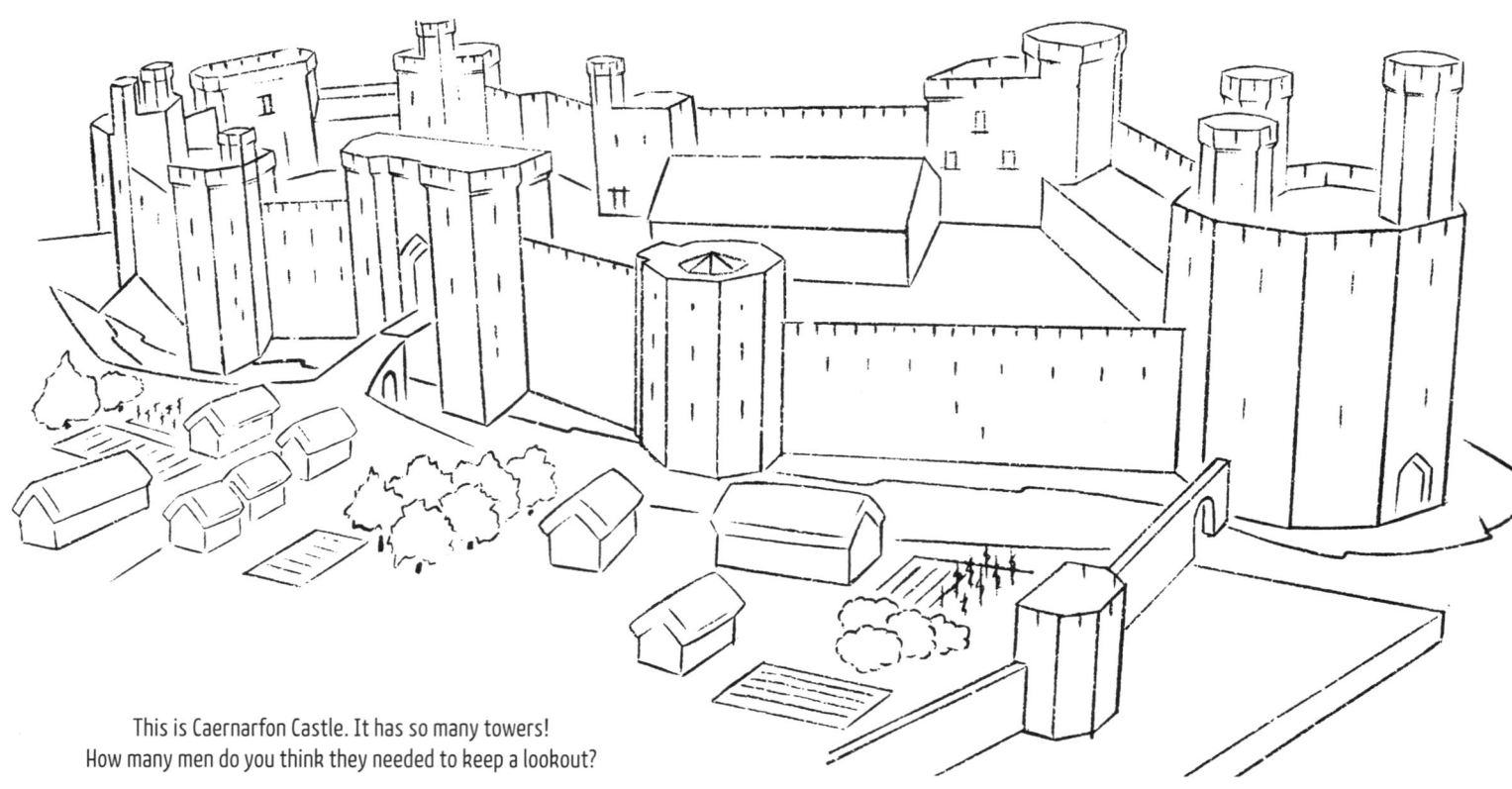

This is Caernarfon Castle. It has so many towers!
How many men do you think they needed to keep a lookout?

Can you build your own castle from recycled materials?

Kitchen roll tubes are great for making towers. You could add a roof, and paint or cut out some windows. Walls can be made from cardboard boxes, with rectangular pieces cut out of the top edge to create the battlements. Small juice cartons are great for buildings such as your great hall, with a roof made from a piece of card or cereal box.

Don't be afraid to experiment – cut things up, and if it doesn't work you can simply put it back in the recycling bin and try again!

You will need:
Cardboard, small boxes, tubes and cartons.
Scissors, glue, pencil, paint, brushes and tape –
masking tape is best as it is easier to glue and paint over.

You may need an adult to help you.

Begin with a large sheet of cardboard to create a base for your model.

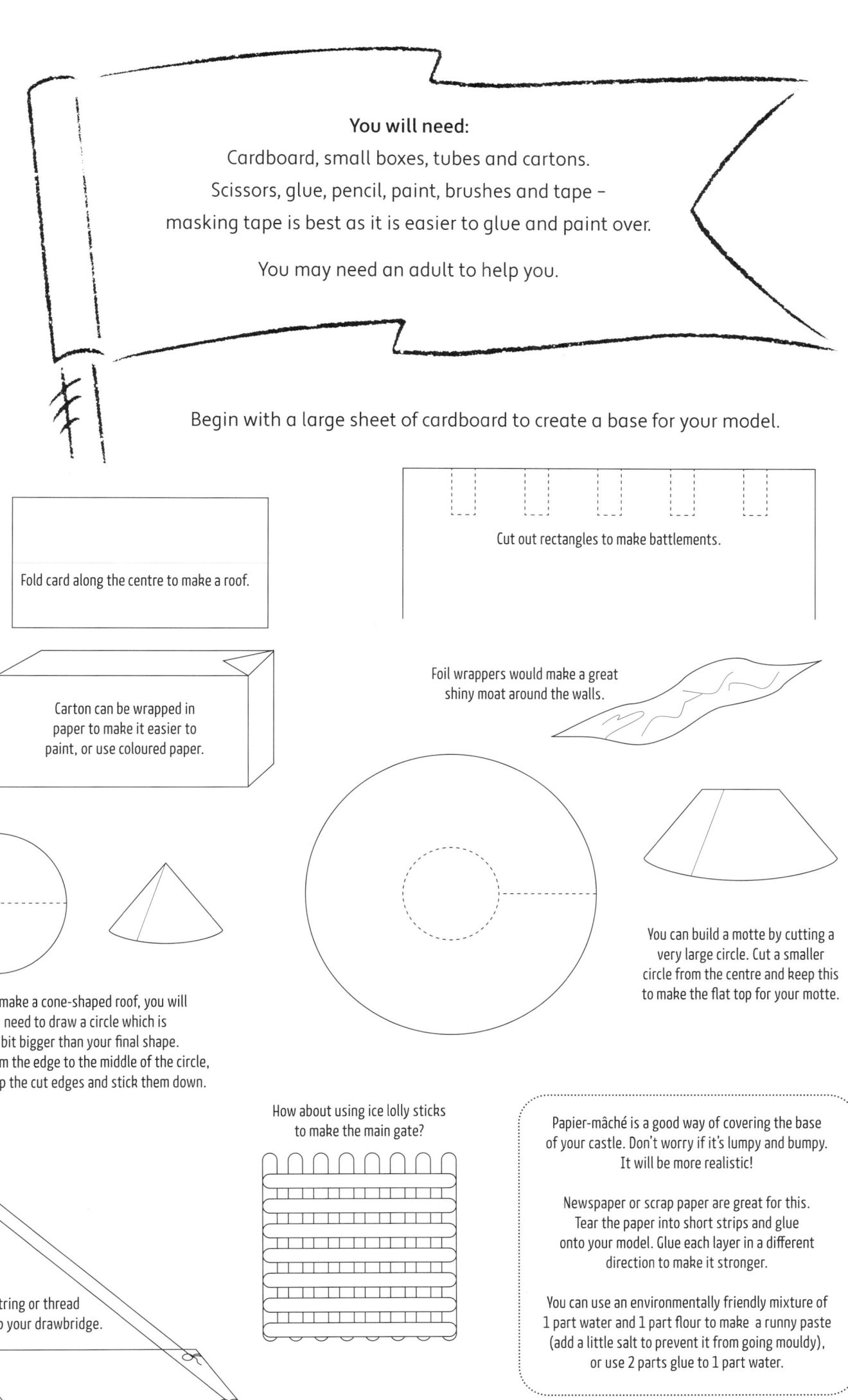

Fold card along the centre to make a roof.

Cut out rectangles to make battlements.

Carton can be wrapped in paper to make it easier to paint, or use coloured paper.

Foil wrappers would make a great shiny moat around the walls.

To make a cone-shaped roof, you will need to draw a circle which is a bit bigger than your final shape. Cut from the edge to the middle of the circle, overlap the cut edges and stick them down.

You can build a motte by cutting a very large circle. Cut a smaller circle from the centre and keep this to make the flat top for your motte.

How about using ice lolly sticks to make the main gate?

Use string or thread to hold up your drawbridge.

Papier-mâché is a good way of covering the base of your castle. Don't worry if it's lumpy and bumpy. It will be more realistic!

Newspaper or scrap paper are great for this. Tear the paper into short strips and glue onto your model. Glue each layer in a different direction to make it stronger.

You can use an environmentally friendly mixture of 1 part water and 1 part flour to make a runny paste (add a little salt to prevent it from going mouldy), or use 2 parts glue to 1 part water.

FUELLING CHANGE

By the middle of the 19th century, during the Industrial Revolution, coal mining became one of the most important industries in Wales. Although coal had been in use for hundreds of years on a small scale – to fuel the blacksmith's forge, for funeral pyres and to heat homes – the invention of steam engines increased the demand for coal to power factories, trains and ships. At the same time, coal replaced charcoal in the process of smelting metals. By the end of the 20th century, there was less coal left in the ground and other sources of fuel became cheaper to use.

Colour in the numbers. What am I?

1 = BLUE
2 = GREEN
3 = DARK GREEN
4 = GOLD/YELLOW
5 = LIGHT BROWN
6 = DARK BROWN
7 = RED
8 = BLACK
9 = GREY

The industrial era brought with it lots of development and new technologies, which improved people's standard of living. It also brought more pollution. We can help make things better by choosing to use sustainable sources of fuel and energy and buying energy-efficient products when we shop.

You can measure your impact on the environment by calculating your carbon footprint. This is worked out from the carbon dioxide (CO_2) emissions of the fuel or energy and products you use.

How big are these carbon footprints per passenger?
Can you number them from 1 to 7, from low to high? (Assume that the vehicles are full.)

- ◯ Plane
- ◯ Car
- ◯ Diesel train
- ◯ Walking
- ◯ Electric train
- ◯ Cycling
- ◯ Bus

The average hot air balloon can hold 5 tonnes (5,000 kg) of CO_2.

There are around 11 tonnes of CO_2 emissions for each person living in Wales.

Answers on page 31.

WALES AND BEYOND

Before lorries were invented, drovers' roads were used to walk livestock to market hundreds of miles away. Goods including cloth, coal, iron, steel, copper and slate, were carried by horse and cart.

PORT PENRHYN – from where slate was exported

BETHESDA

PENRHYN SLATE QUARRY

This light railway connected the Penrhyn Slate Quarry near Bethesda with the dock at Port Penrhyn on the Menai Strait.

RIVER TAFF

CARDIFF BAY

The River Taff runs into Cardiff Bay where a series of docks was built to load and unload the ships.

There was a large network of canals in south Wales, connecting major towns and industries with the docks. Some of these are still there today, but transporting goods is now mainly done by lorries.

BRECON
MERTHYR TYDFIL
BURRY PORT
ABERDARE
NEWPORT
PORT TALBOT
CARDIFF

Throughout Wales, many canals, tramlines and railways were built to transport goods more easily. These networks often carried the goods straight to the ports where they were put on ships and exported all over the world. This included shipping millions of tonnes of slate to the West Indies, the United States of America, Argentina, South Africa, Europe and Australia.

GWR stands for the "Great Western Railway", the company that ran most of the train lines in Wales at one time.

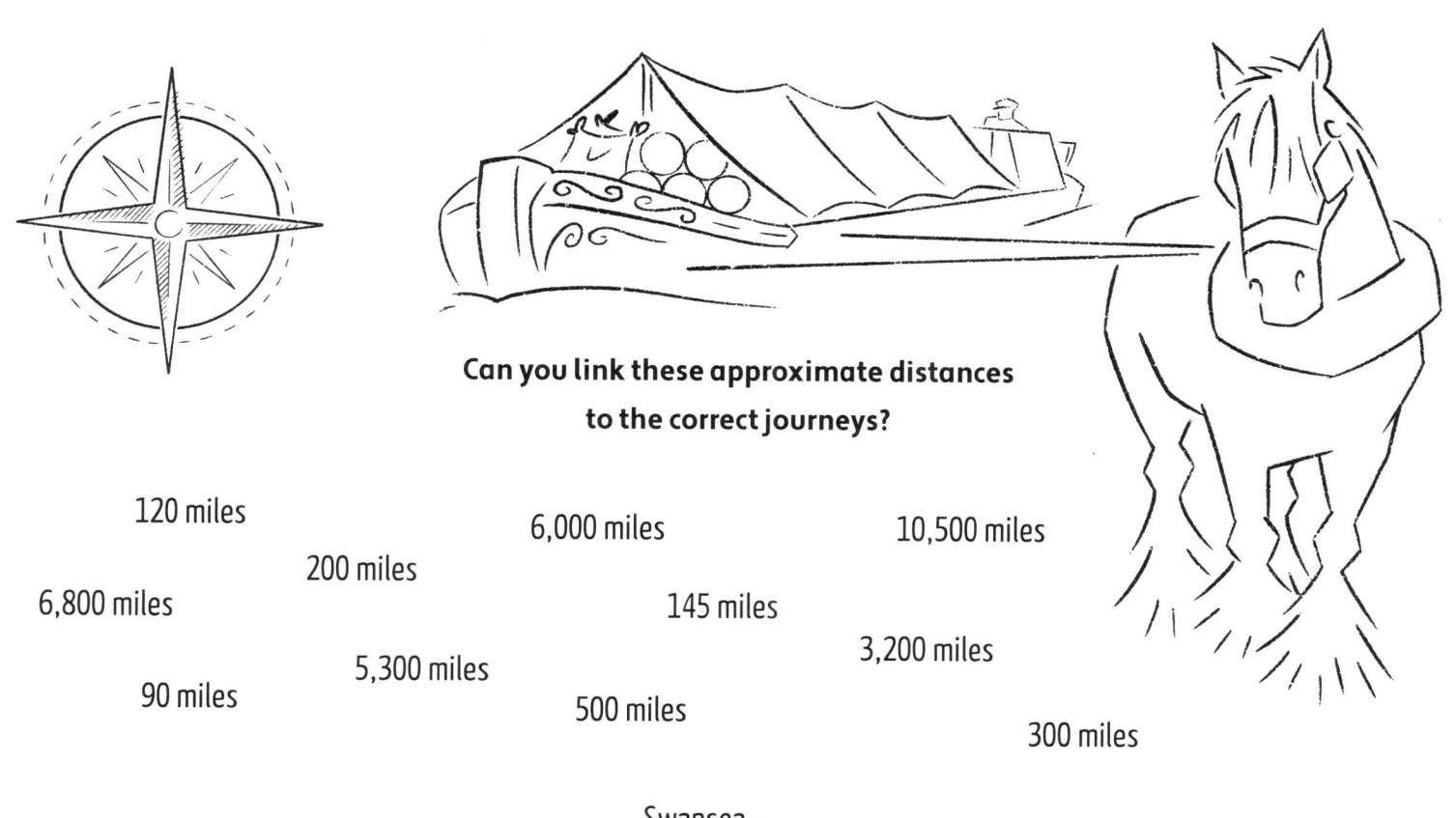

Can you link these approximate distances to the correct journeys?

120 miles   6,000 miles   10,500 miles

200 miles

6,800 miles   145 miles

        5,300 miles   3,200 miles

90 miles

        500 miles

                300 miles

Swansea – Buenos Aires, Argentina

Broughton, Flintshire – Llanelli, Carmarthenshire

Porthmadog, Gwynedd – Los Angeles, USA

Llandovery, Carmarthenshire – Smithfield Market, London, England

Blaenau Ffestiniog, Gwynedd – New South Wales, Australia

Cardiff – Cape Town, South Africa

Llanddeusant, Anglesey – Manchester, England

Pembroke Dock, Pembrokeshire – Bordeaux, France

Little Newcastle, Pembrokeshire – Ivory Coast

Bethesda, Gwynedd – Dublin, Ireland

Aberystwyth, Ceredigion – Edinburgh, Scotland

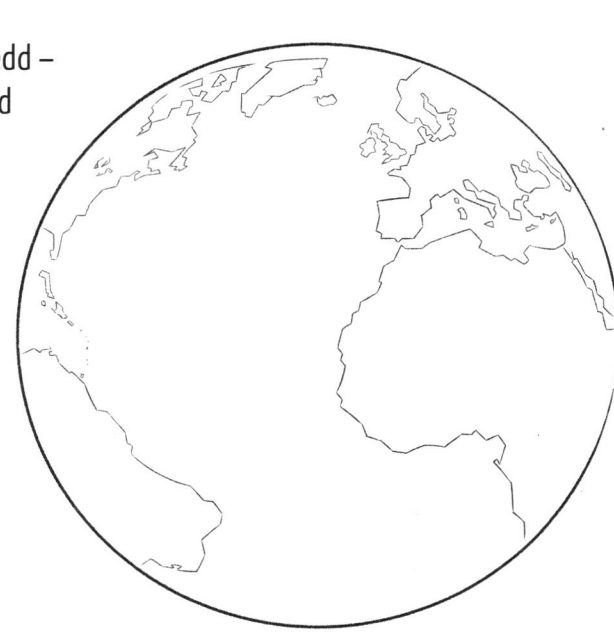

Answers on page 31.

PROTEST! PROTEST!

Protest is an important way of standing up for your rights, a way to try and make life better and fairer for you and for others. From working hours to equal pay, the right to vote and climate change, protest has had a direct impact on how we live today.

Can you come up with your own slogans?

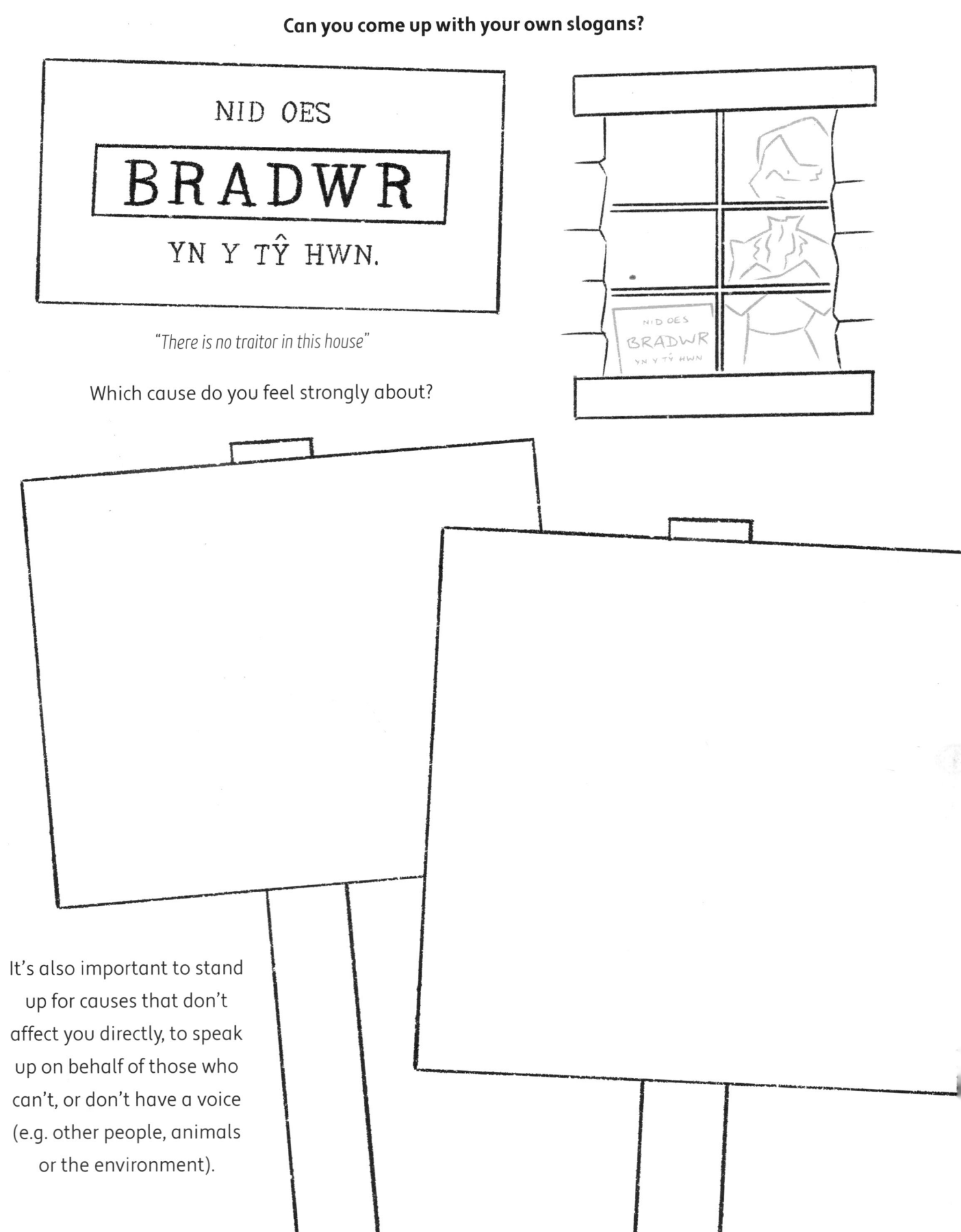

NID OES **BRADWR** YN Y TŶ HWN.

"There is no traitor in this house"

Which cause do you feel strongly about?

It's also important to stand up for causes that don't affect you directly, to speak up on behalf of those who can't, or don't have a voice (e.g. other people, animals or the environment).

GOVERNMENT

Life today is a lot fairer than it used to be, for example women have been given the right to vote, as well as men, and treating someone differently because of their race is illegal. But there is always room to improve. A manifesto describes what a political party or candidate believes in and what they want to do or change if they win an election.

Imagine you are a candidate standing for election as school president. What would be in your manifesto? Can you design a poster or leaflet to tell everyone about it?

....
....
....

**Some laws made perfect sense at the time, but seem ridiculous to us today...
Can you tell which of these 13 statements are true or false?**

A Welshman had to pay 12 pence to enter the City of London.

It was illegal to eat leeks for breakfast.

It was illegal for a woman to eat chocolate on a bus.

Children were not allowed to wear armour.

You must not put a pig on a lead.

Welsh people were not allowed to carry any arms into Chester, apart from a knife to eat with.

It's illegal to have a pigsty in front of your house.

It was illegal for a man to sing in a barn.

A cat that had killed mice was worth four pence.

You must not hang a washing line across a street.

It's illegal to keep cows as pets.

It was illegal to keep crows as pets.

If you murdered someone, you had to pay compensation to their family.

Answers on page 32.

There are many different forms of government. In the past, Wales was ruled by powerful people who could often do as they pleased. But today we live in a democracy. We are lucky that we can vote for people to stand up for us, and have a say in how our country is run.

P	A	R	C	D	E	M	O	P	W	Y	P	T	U	M	O	B	I	E	P
E	X	A	K	B	L	W	C	E	P	A	R	P	A	R	L	I	P	Z	O
A	L	R	O	S	E	A	V	T	C	R	L	N	Q	A	X	E	N	T	I
M	O	T	A	C	P	P	A	R	L	I	A	M	E	N	T	G	F	Y
O	T	Y	P	O	T	A	E	B	C	F	G	N	W	T	K	O	B	E	C
P	E	Q	U	V	I	M	B	D	E	R	V	R	C	R	V	E	S	S	A
R	A	N	E	T	O	V	X	S	N	W	O	A	W	E	I	P	M	O	R
A	I	R	R	F	N	I	T	L	E	A	D	E	R	D	M	Z	E	R	C
M	W	A	T	A	P	O	R	M	F	S	C	N	U	E	A	F	T	L	O
X	C	I	C	Y	E	X	Y	L	R	A	M	A	S	L	P	N	A	W	M
Y	Z	Y	P	A	S	I	A	E	B	E	D	W	N	O	F	Y	D	T	E
T	F	L	A	W	S	P	D	F	N	S	E	N	M	P	R	I	E	N	D
P	E	B	S	P	A	A	C	T	A	U	V	A	O	A	G	Q	V	U	I
A	D	M	A	G	O	V	R	I	T	D	U	T	G	U	N	W	O	R	C
S	W	E	N	W	P	L	Q	C	L	W	L	I	E	I	X	I	L	P	E
B	I	S	C	A	N	D	I	D	A	T	E	O	D	F	S	T	U	M	I
N	W	S	O	Z	U	A	K	T	P	Q	D	N	E	P	B	E	T	R	P
A	B	A	L	E	G	O	E	X	I	T	A	A	S	S	E	M	I	E	V
U	L	O	P	Y	R	T	N	U	O	C	R	L	B	Z	S	A	O	K	O
O	R	G	N	A	M	E	V	E	L	T	S	A	T	A	S	O	N	A	G

Where are these words hiding?

Act — Devolution — National
Assembly — Election — Parliament
Candidate — Government — Party
Country — Laws — Politics
Crown — Leader — Prince
Democracy — Manifesto — Vote

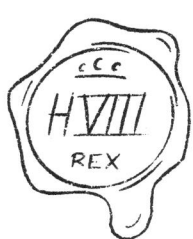

Answers on page 32.

23

INVENTIVE WALES

There are many inventions which started out in Wales.
Here are some in the field of science and technology:

William Robert Grove invented the first fuel cell, now more commonly known as a battery.

William Frost designed an early flying machine, the "Frost Airship Glider", which flew about 500 metres in 1896.

Draw your own invention below.

Name your machine, briefly describe what it does and don't forget to label the diagram!

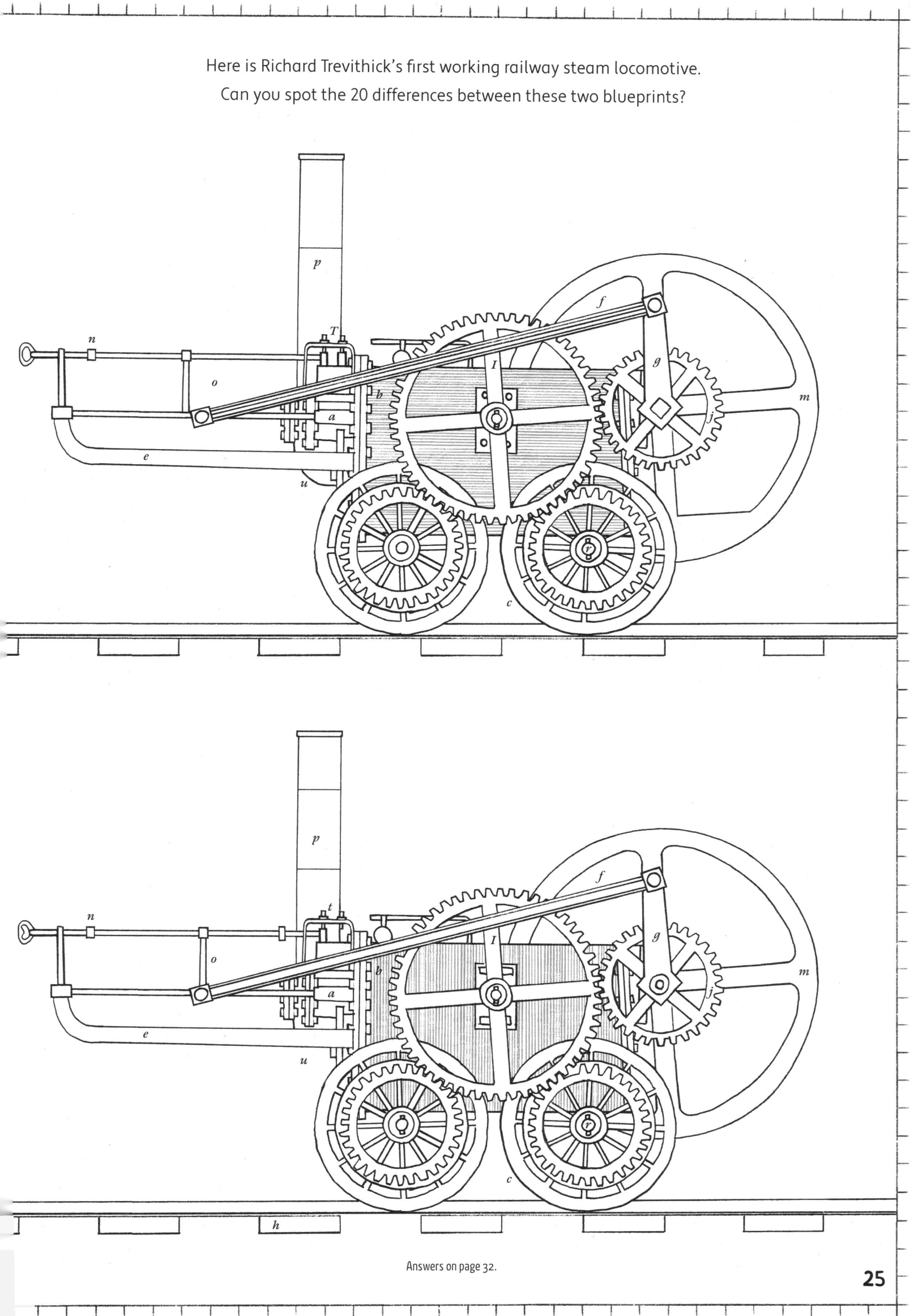

Here is Richard Trevithick's first working railway steam locomotive.
Can you spot the 20 differences between these two blueprints?

Answers on page 32.

25

TIME MACHINE

If you could travel back to a period in history, which one would you choose?
Set your controls, draw the hands on your dials and slide the lever to GO!
How about writing the story of your journey through time?

My destination

10 Stories in Welsh History Time Machine – Patent Pending 2021.
The author cannot be held responsible for any mishaps that occur during use.
Readers maintain responsibility for their own adventures at all times.

TIMELINE QUIZ

How much do you know about Welsh history? See if you can answer the questions below, then look at the poster in the back of the book to learn more details.

1. The first known human in Wales, whose bones were found in Gower, lived:
   a) 6 billion years BCE
   b) 82 million years BCE
   c) 33 thousand years BCE
   d) 101 CE

2. During the Bronze Age, people made tools out of bronze. But which metal is the main ingredient of bronze?
   a) Gold
   b) Titanium
   c) Iron
   d) Copper

3. Where did the Normans build their first castle in Wales?
   a) Chepstow
   b) Hereford
   c) Aberystwyth
   d) Flint

4. Offa's Dyke was built to:
   a) Hold back the Irish Sea
   b) Mark the border between Powys and Mercia
   c) As a raised road for soldiers to march along
   d) To stop livestock escaping

5. Llywelyn the Great's real name was:
   a) Llywelyn ap Cadell
   b) Llywelyn ap Gruffudd
   c) Llywelyn ap Hywel
   d) Llywelyn ap Iorwerth

6. What percentage of the population of Wales died from the Black Death in 1348?
   a) Around 14%
   b) Around 23%
   c) Around 30%
   d) Around 42%

7. Which army sailed to Pembrokeshire and launched an invasion in 1797?
   a) English
   b) French
   c) German
   d) Spanish

8. What did the Chartists do?
   a) Fought for votes for all working men
   b) They charted the first maps of Wales
   c) Wrote down everyone's names for the census
   d) Drew family tree charts to prove how important people were

9. The first National Eisteddfod took place in:
   a) Aberdare
   b) Bangor
   c) Llanuwchllyn
   d) Tregaron

10. How many Welsh settlers arrived in Patagonia, South America, in 1865?
    a) 16
    b) 92
    c) 153
    d) 204

11. Llanwddyn was flooded to build Lake Vyrnwy:
    a) To make a fishing lake
    b) To provide water for Liverpool
    c) For boating competitions at the Olympics
    d) To prevent flooding down river

12. In which year was Cardiff named the capital city of Wales?
    a) 1282
    b) 1642
    c) 1916
    d) 1955

Answers on page 32.

DEAR DIARY...

Write a diary entry describing your experiences of a particular event, for example, the Saint David's Day celebrations at your school, or your visit to the Eisteddfod.

Things that have happened in the past help to shape the world we live in, and make us who we are today. By writing down your story today, you are helping to write history and you might help someone in the future understand what happened.

Original records of our history, that were made by people who lived through an event, are called primary sources. These are first-hand or eyewitness accounts and information, provided by people who were actually there. For example a diary, letter or photograph.

Historians, who study the past, can use these sources today to find out what people saw, heard, and thought at the time. In the past, historians, writing after the event, might give a different view of what happened, depending on their political opinion, or the way people felt at the time they were writing the history.

Don't forget:

Time

Diaries start with a date, day of the week and sometimes the time they were written.

Order

Usually written in chronological order, so write about things in the order in which they happened.

First person

You are writing about yourself, so remember to use "me", or "I"...

Here is an example of a diary entry:

Friday, 1st March

I was so excited when I woke up this morning, I jumped out of bed and ran downstairs. My big sister was already wearing her Welsh lady outfit, but didn't look too pleased about it. I loved my clothes. With my waistcoat and cap on I looked so smart. As we were leaving for school, Mam picked us a daffodil each from the garden and pinned them to our chests.

Assembly is normally so boring, but today Mr Jones told us the story of St. David and then we all sang Hen Wlad fy Nhadau. My best friend, Jac, sang louder than anyone, proudly wearing a red rugby shirt. We spent all morning drawing loads of dragons and making flags, before the photographer from the local newspaper came to take a picture of us all together in our fancy dress.

We had leek and potato soup for lunch, the same as every year. Then it was some maths work, which I obviously love, before we had to finish getting everything ready for the St. David's Day parade which will be held in town tomorrow.

When I got home from school, the house was full of an amazing smell. Dad had been busy cooking and there were so many Welsh cakes it was like a mountain on the plate. But by the time Mam came home from work, there were barely any left!

I'm stuffed now. I have to go to bed early so I won't be too tired at the parade. Can't wait to see all my friends there.

Nos da!

OH, HOW HAPPY I AM...

Poems are a great way of expressing how you feel, and they can also tell us a story. Writers can re-tell a story in their own words and tell us what they think happened. When we are looking back at historical events, these are known as secondary sources and can help us understand how people felt at the time.

Before people could write things down, they depended on word of mouth. They passed on their history by telling stories and poems, and singing songs. This "spoken history" was written down later in a book or a set of poems. For example, the famous Red Book of Hergest is a large manuscript written in 1382. This was before paper was invented, so the pages are made out of vellum, animal skin stretched out thinly.

> **Can you write a poem to describe something that happened to you?**
> Poems tend to describe our emotions and feelings. Think of something that made you really, really happy and write down what happened and how you felt.

These are some things to consider when you write your poem:

Write anything
Just get your ideas written down first, without thinking too much. Even the best poets will cut, add and change their poems to make them better as they go along.

Length
A poem can be a few short lines, or as long as a book.

Rhyming
Poems don't have to rhyme, but it can help add rhythm to your poem.

Paint a picture with words
Help the readers imagine themselves in your shoes.

Metaphors
e.g. The boat sailed over *the mirror* of water.

Similies
e.g. The sun was *like* a giant egg yolk.

Have fun!
You will always write your best poem when you're having fun, or writing about something that you love.

ANSWERS

Page 4–5
WHO'S WHO?
7. Alfred Russel Wallace
2. Abram Wood
3. Betty Campbell
11. Black Bart
13. Dic Penderyn
6. Eileen Beasley
1. Frances Hoggan
5. Gwenllian ferch Gruffudd
10. Henry Morgan
9. Joan Curran
4. Lyn Evans
8. Owain Glyndŵr
12. Margaret Tisdale
14. Mr Urdd

Page 6–7
WHICH HAPPENED FIRST?
1. 1952
2. 1415
3. 1858
4. 1919
5. 948
6. 2001
7. 1884
8. 1839
9. 1258
10. c. 1100
11. 1999
12. 1991
13. 1672
14. 1966
15. 1176

Page 9
MATHEMOOTICS
- One cow produces 1,500 litres of slurry every 30 days
- The farmer needs to have enough storage space for 6,000 litres of slurry per cow.
- The average dairy herd produces 570,000 litres of slurry over 120 days.
- The average cow would provide milk for 45,000 bowls of cereal.
- One person having a bowl of cereal each day for a year would use 73 litres of milk.
- Jac takes 30ml of milk a day in his tea.
- Sioned takes 200ml of milk a day in her tea.
- Bethan takes 60ml of milk a day in her tea.
- Mei takes 150ml of milk a day in his coffee.

Page 8
FARMING

Page 12–13
DEFENDING WALES
1. Parapet
2. Battlement
3. Keep
4. Palisade
5. Great Hall
6. Bailey
7. Main Gate
8. Motte
9. Scarp
10. Ditch or Moat
11. Curtain Wall
12. Drawbridge

PAGE 17
FUELLING CHANGE
CO_2 emissions listed per kilometre, per passenger.

1. Cycling = 0.14g
2. Walking = 0.26g
3. Bus = 18g
4. Electric train = 20g
5. Diesel Train = 29g
6. Car with x 5 passengers = 48g
7. Plane
   - Flight under 1 hour = 150g
   - Flight 1-5 hours = 240g
   - Flight over 5 hours = 320g

The average car will produce 240g of CO_2 per km. This means that a car with only one passenger has the same carbon footprint as a plane!

PAGE 19
WALES AND BEYOND
90	Bethesda, Gwynedd – Dublin, Ireland
120	Llanddeusant, Anglesey – Manchester, England
145	Broughton, Flintshire – Llanelli, Carmarthenshire
200	Llandovery, Carmarthenshire – Smithfield Market, London, England
300	Aberystwyth, Ceredigion – Edinburgh, Scotland
500	Pembroke Dock, Pembrokeshire – Bordeaux, France
3,200	Little Newcastle, Pembrokeshire – Ivory Coast
5,300	Porthmadog, Gwynedd – Los Angeles, USA
6,000	Cardiff – Cape Town, South Africa
6,800	Swansea – Buenos Aires, Argentina
10,500	Blaenau Ffestiniog, Gwynedd – New South Wales, Australia

PAGE 22
GOVERNMENT – TRUE OR FALSE
FALSE – A Welshman had to pay 12 pence to enter the City of London.
FALSE – It was illegal to eat leeks for breakfast.
FALSE – Children were not allowed to wear armour.
TRUE – It was illegal for a woman to eat chocolate on a bus.
FALSE – You must not put a pig on a lead.
TRUE – Welsh people were not allowed to carry any arms into Chester, apart from a knife to eat with.
TRUE – It's illegal to have a pigsty in front of your house.
FALSE – It was illegal for a man to sing in a barn.
TRUE – A cat that had killed mice was worth four pence.
TRUE – You must not hang a washing line across a street.
TRUE – It's illegal to keep cows as pets.
FALSE – It was illegal to keep crows as pets.
TRUE – If you murdered someone, you had to pay compensation to their family.

PAGE 23
GOVERNMENT – WORDSEARCH
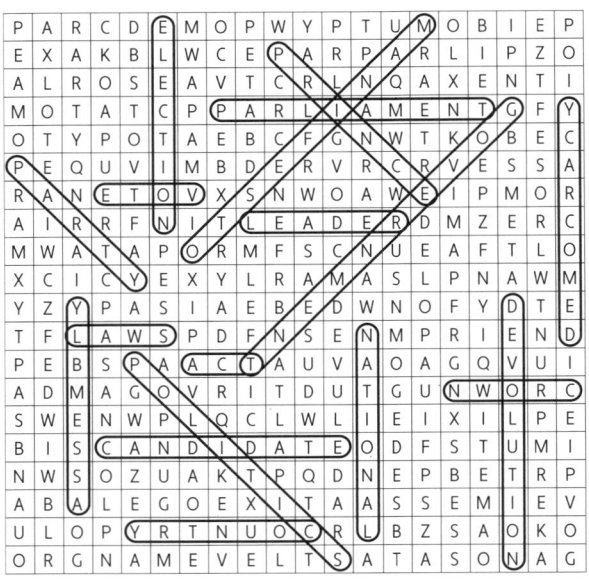

PAGE 25
INVENTIVE WALES – SPOT THE DIFFERENCE
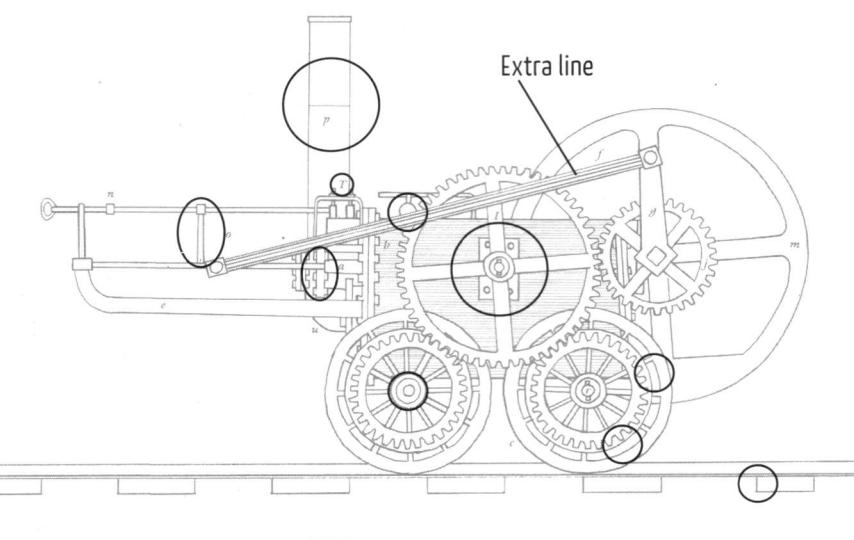
Extra line

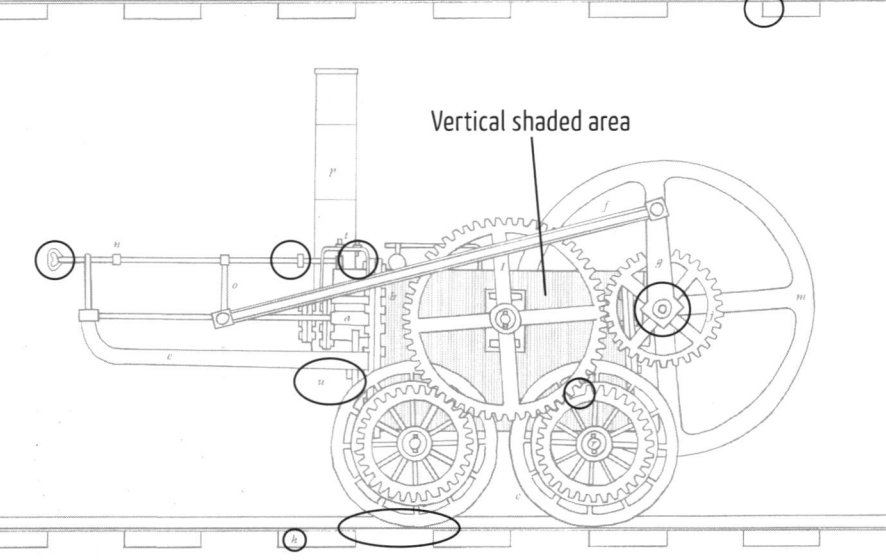
Vertical shaded area

PAGE 27
TIMELINE QUIZ
1. c) 33 thousand years BCE
2. d) Copper
3. a) Chepstow
4. b) Mark the border between Powys and Mercia
5. d) Llywelyn ap Iorwerth
6. c) Around 30%
7. b) French
8. a) Fought for votes for all working men
9. a) Aberdare
10. c) 153
11. b) To provide water for Liverpool
12. d) 1955

The publishers would like to thank Ifan Morgan Jones, Alun Morgan, Eleri Huws and the editor Siân Lewis for their support.

Published by Dragon Press 2021
An imprint of Rily Publications Ltd,
PO Box 257, Caerphilly CF83 9FL

ISBN 978-1-84967-544-4

Text © Tanwen Haf, 2021
Illustrations © Telor Gwyn, 2021 / except for:
cover & page 1: time machines;
pages, 9 t, cl, bl; 10; 15, 17 tr, cl, cr; 25-26;
29-30 bg. © Tanwen Haf, 2021
Design by Tanwen Haf, Whitefire Designs
Characters, Concept and Storyline © HRDT Ltd 2021

The right of Tanwen Haf and Telor Gwyn to be identified as the author and illustrator of this Work has been asserted by them in accordance with sections 77 and 78 of the Copyright, Designs and Patents Act 1988.

All rights reserved under International and Pan-American Copyright Conventions. No part of this publication may be reproduced, distributed stored or transmitted in any form, or by any means, without the prior written permission of the publisher.

Dragon Press has made every reasonable effort to ensure that any picture content and written content in this book has been included or removed in accordance with the contractual and technological constraints in operation at the time of publication.

Published with the financial support of the Books Council of Wales.

Printed in Wales.

dragonpress.co.uk